R0202361812

09/2021

W9-BBT-611

Dear Parents:

Congratulations! Your child is taking the first steps on an exciting journey. The destination? Independent reading!

STEP INTO READING® will help your child get there. The program offers five steps to reading success. Each step includes fun stories and colorful art or photographs. In addition to original fiction and books with favorite characters, there are Step into Reading Non-Fiction Readers, Phonics Readers and Boxed Sets, Sticker Readers, and Comic Readers—a complete literacy program with something to interest every child.

Learning to Read, Step by Step!

Ready to Read   Preschool–Kindergarten
• big type and easy words • rhyme and rhythm • picture clues
For children who know the alphabet and are eager to begin reading.

Reading with Help   Preschool–Grade 1
• basic vocabulary • short sentences • simple stories
For children who recognize familiar words and sound out new words with help.

Reading on Your Own   Grades 1–3
• engaging characters • easy-to-follow plots • popular topics
For children who are ready to read on their own.

Reading Paragraphs   Grades 2–3
• challenging vocabulary • short paragraphs • exciting stories
For newly independent readers who read simple sentences with confidence.

Ready for Chapters   Grades 2–4
• chapters • longer paragraphs • full-color art
For children who want to take the plunge into chapter books but still like colorful pictures.

STEP INTO READING® is designed to give every child a successful reading experience. The grade levels are only guides; children will progress through the steps at their own speed, developing confidence in their reading. The F&P Text Level on the back cover serves as another tool to help you choose the right book for your child.

Remember, a lifetime love of reading starts with a single step!

Text and illustrations copyright © 2012 by John Bemelmans Marciano
Character of Madeline copyright © 2012 by Ludwig Bemelmans, LLC

Visit us on the Web!
StepIntoReading.com
rhcbooks.com

Educators and librarians, for a variety of teaching tools, visit us at RHTeachersLibrarians.com

Library of Congress Cataloging-in-Publication Data is available upon request.
ISBN 978-0-593-43238-9 (trade) — ISBN 978-0-593-43239-6 (lib. bdg.)

Printed in the United States of America
10 9 8 7 6 5 4 3 2 1

This book has been officially leveled by using the F&P Text Level Gradient™ Leveling System.

MADELINE'S
TEA PARTY

by John Bemelmans Marciano
illustrated by JT Morrow
based on the art of John Bemelmans Marciano

Random House 🏠 New York

In an old house in Paris

that is covered with vines,

live twelve little girls

in two straight lines.

They leave the house

at half past nine.

The smallest one is Madeline.

Madeline is hosting

an afternoon tea.

The party begins at half past three.

The girls come in

all smartly dressed.

Each one wears her Sunday best.

One last guest is very late.

The girls must sit and wait

and wait.

At last, at almost half past four,

a most selfish boy strolls

through the door.

He won't say he's sorry

or take off his hat.

But that is Pepito,

the world's greatest brat.

Madeline fills each cup with tea.

The girls drink it up

most happily.

Pepito takes a sip.

He makes a face.

He spits out tea

all over the place.

"This party stinks!" he says.

"But you know what's fun?

Magic tricks—I'll show you one!"

"Watch how

the amazing Pepito is able

to remove the cloth out

from this table!"

But his magic skills are fake!

The cups all fly around

and break.

The bad hat laughs.

The girls are sad.

Now Madeline is really mad.

"If you can't behave in

a proper way,

please, Pepito, GO AWAY!"

"Fine!" he says.

"I don't want to stay.

It's a silly party, anyway!"

He starts to leave

but in comes a cake.

Maybe Pepito made a mistake!

The cake is a surprise

from Madeline's father.

The girls all cheer

and hug each other.

As the cake is cut,

the boy's heart sinks.

"I should have been nicer,"

Pepito thinks.

He is followed home

by a cloud of gloom.

Now Pepito cries

alone in his room.

Then he hears the *bing-bang-bong*

of the doorbell's mighty gong.

He sees Madeline at the door.

But what has *she* come here for?

"There was an extra slice of cake
I thought that you might like to take."

Pepito looks up, down,

and all around.

He kicks a rock lying

on the ground.

He says, "I'm sorry

for how I behaved before.

I promise not to be

such a brat anymore."

Pepito thanks Madeline

for the lovely treat.

And the two good friends

sit down to eat.